RollerCoaster TYCOON

Pick Your Path!

Sudden Turn

For my two families—
the Breauxs,
who kept my feet on the ground,
and the Broussards,
who kept my head in the clouds.—S.B.

ISBN 0-439-49152-5

12 11 10 9 8 7 6 5 4 3 2   2 3 4 5 6 7/0

Printed in the U.S.A.   40

First Scholastic printing, November 2002

Sudden Turn

By Shane Breaux
Cover illustration by Neil Stewart

SCHOLASTIC INC.
New York Toronto London Auckland Sydney
Mexico City New Delhi Hong Kong Buenos Aires

Marty Butterfield walked into his house, dropped his backpack by the door, and headed straight to the kitchen. He grabbed a cookie, then spotted something on the kitchen table that caught his eye—an envelope sealed with red wax.

"What's this?" Marty wondered, picking it up. It was addressed to his sister, Megnolia. The wax seal on the back was stamped with a "B," which could only mean one thing: it was from their great-grandmother, Big Bonnie.

All the women in their family were named Bonnie, after their great-grandmother. That's why she was called Big Bonnie. Megnolia was named Bonnie, too, but she chose to use her middle name instead. She hated to be called Bonnie, or even Meg for short. She was *Megnolia,* thank you very much!

Marty didn't have to deal with any names being passed down to him, and he was happy about that. But he was *unhappy* that Megnolia had gotten a letter from Big Bonnie and he had not.

Marty and Megnolia were close in age, but they were total opposites. Marty was a vegetarian, while Megnolia drooled at the sight of meat. Megnolia passed her time doing science experiments, and Marty spent every spare minute watching horror movies.

The only thing they shared was their passion for

roller coasters. They both belonged to the Coaster Crazies Club, and for the past few years, they had been saving their money to go on a theme park tour of the country. They planned to visit every big park and ride all the major rides.

Megnolia was due home anytime now, and Marty couldn't wait to find out what Big Bonnie had to say to Megnolia that she couldn't say to him, too. He sat at the kitchen table, turning the envelope in his hands. That's when he noticed the corner of another envelope sticking out of the summer double issue of *Coasters Illustrated.* Could it be?

Sure enough, the envelope was addressed to him. Marty tore it open and read the letter:

Dearest Marty,

    I have just sold my share of the family puzzle factory, and I'd like to give you and Megnolia a piece of the family fortune. You may use the money as you wish. I only require that whatever you choose to do with the money lives up to the Butterfield name and that you follow your dreams. I will send the check soon.

               Dream big,
               Big Bonnie

Marty stared at the letter, stunned. He was about to start jumping up and down like an idiot when his sister walked into the room.

"You should see this wild mold I'm growing in science class," Megnolia was saying, but she stopped when she saw Marty's face. "Hey, what's the matter?"

Marty handed his sister her letter.

"From Big Bonnie?" Megnolia said. "What does it say?"

"You won't believe it," Marty said, shaking his head.

Megnolia ripped open her letter and read it on the spot. Soon she and Marty were *both* jumping up and down like idiots.

"This is awesome!" Megnolia shouted. "Do you know what this means? We can start our theme park tour now!"

"Are you kidding?" Marty replied. "We could use the money to open our *own* parks! If we combine our cash, we can build the biggest park ever."

Megnolia smiled. "I love it!" she said. "You know what would be the perfect spot? That huge flat area downtown. We could dig a big crater there and fill it with water to make a lake. Then we could build adventure rides all around it!"

"Well, that sounds *cute*, I guess, but I think we could do much better," Marty said.

Megnolia's smile faded. "Oh yeah? What could be better than that?"

Marty grabbed a pencil and started scribbling on the back of his envelope. "I think we should build it over a lake *outside* of town," Marty said. "We can create an icy landscape so it's like you've traveled to the North Pole."

"Great," said Megnolia. "Then all of our theme park guests will get frostbite. What fun!"

"That's better than sticking a park in a stupid crater!" Marty shot back.

"What's stupid is your idea!" Megnolia yelled.

"Well you're just a—" Marty stopped himself. He must have been crazy thinking he and his sister could build a park together. They couldn't even agree on what to eat for dinner. How could they ever agree on a whole park?

"Tell you what," Marty said. "Why don't you take your money and build your silly crater park? I'll build my own park—without you!"

"Fine!" Megnolia shouted. "We'll see whose park is better."

Megnolia turned around, stormed through the door, and slammed it behind her. The contest had begun!

- To build a park with Marty,
  go to page 98.
- To build a park with Megnolia,
  go to page 29.

"Forget about kiddie rides," Marty told Stanley. "I am going to design my very first coaster. I don't care if I use up my cash. This coaster is going to be so great, it's guaranteed to bring in tons of money."

Stanley swallowed a piece of pretzel. "Would you make it a looping coaster for me? With a powerful launch system, so the cars zoom up the hill really fast?"

"Absolutely!" Marty was psyched to build a ride, especially for his friend. Owning a theme park was turning out to be the coolest job ever!

He designed the coaster with three loops and a top speed of sixty miles per hour.

"Cool!" Stanley said, looking up at the ride. "It looks like a giant pretzel. A frosted pretzel!"

"Then that's what we'll call it," Marty said.

The Frosted Pretzel became a gigantic smash hit. The crowds swarmed Iceberg Islands, and the money started pouring in. Once again, Marty had plenty of extra cash to play around with.

"Tycooning isn't all that tough," he thought. That's when his cell phone rang.

"Hello," Marty said.

"*Bonjour.* This is Monsieur Poulet," said the voice on the phone in a French accent. "I am calling on behalf of Michael Georges."

"Are you kidding me? Michael Georges? MG, the greatest coaster designer alive?" Marty asked. He couldn't believe it.

"*Oui.* No joke."

Marty put his hand over the phone receiver. "Hey, Stanley! MG's people are on the phone—for *me!*"

"Whoa, Chief!" Stanley exclaimed.

Marty pulled himself together. "This is Marty Butterfield. How can you help me—I mean, how can I—I mean, *I can't believe MG wants to talk to me!*" Marty couldn't hold in his excitement any longer.

Monsieur Poulet cleared his throat. "Well, you see, Monsieur Georges has visited your park on several occasions. Undercover, of course. And he loves it. He wants to know if you would like him to design a coaster *pour vous?*"

Just to ride a coaster of MG's would have been an incredible honor for Marty. And now MG wanted to design one for his park! It was almost too much for Marty to handle.

But Marty gathered his wits quickly. "That might be possible. Let me put you through to my people." He handed the phone to Stanley.

"Uh. Mmm. We'd love it," Stanley said.

"Fantasteeck!" Monsieur Poulet said. "There is

one other thing. Monsieur Georges has ridden the Frosted Pretzel. He is very impressed. He wants to know if Monsieur Butterfield would like to collaborate on the coaster with him. If not, Monsieur Georges has a new idea for a major coaster he would like to work on himself. But he demands that you give him absolute free reign."

"Uh, Monsoon Butterfield will have to call you back," Stanley said, and hung up.

- **What should Marty do? If Marty lets MG design the coaster on his own, go to page 92.**

- **If he decides to collaborate with MG, go to page 48.**

"Star Crunch, I think you're on to something," she said. "Puke pouches are a great gimmick, and people love gimmicks!"

Megnolia had twenty-five thousand pouches printed up right away and sold them for a dollar each. Each bag read, "Crater Lake is so exciting, even the Carousel makes you puke!" Megnolia used the slogan on newspaper ads, too.

People started talking about Crater Lake. Soon it became a challenge to see if you could hold on to your cookies while on the rides.

"I ain't afraid of no puke!" one young man bragged.

Megnolia was having fun. She sold T-shirts and hosted an endurance contest. The winner rode Bonnie's Comet nine times in a row without puking once! Megnolia gave her a trophy shaped like a puke pouch. The contest was a hit! Megnolia made them a weekly event.

Megnolia was going over her growing budget one day when the phone rang. She picked up the receiver.

"Megnolia!" It was her brother, Marty.

Megnolia couldn't believe it. She'd barely spoken to her brother since they'd fought about what kind of park to create.

"Are you calling to admit I was right?" Megnolia asked. "I'm sure you've heard how great my park is doing."

"Actually, my park is doing really great, too," Marty said. "In fact, we're shooting a 3-D movie here right now. I wanted to see if you wanted to merge our parks. We could have one big Butterfield theme park!"

Megnolia didn't know how to answer. Merging the parks wasn't a bad idea. The puke pouches were a great gimmick, but the hype they created wouldn't last forever. Merging with Marty could breathe new life into the park.

On the other hand, she would have to work with Marty. Would they actually be able to agree on anything?

- If Megnolia takes the risk and merges parks with Marty, go to page 91.

- If Megnolia refuses Marty's offer, go to page 40.

. . . .

"I'm going to give it a shot. Being a vegetarian is cool—and tasty," Marty said confidently. "You'll see, Stanley. This park has never settled for ordinary."

Stanley tried to be supportive. "Whatever you say, Chief."

Marty went to work right away. He gave up on his tofu-on-a-stick idea—that sounded a little gross even to him. But he opened a few Shamburger huts that sold meatless burgers, two Not Dog stands that sold soy hot dogs, and two pizza parlors that served tofu-roni pizza. He also served meatless lasagna called lasoygna.

When the new Not Dog stands opened, Marty hired actors to dress as pigs and hold signs that read, DON'T EAT ME! EAT A NOT DOG! Outside the Shamburger huts stood happy cows with signs that read, EVEN I'D EAT A SHAMBURGER!

Most of the guests seemed happy to try the food once—and only once.

"Eating tofuroni is like eating glue," Marty heard someone say.

Marty was devastated. He thought the food tasted great, but that didn't matter. He had to shut down most of the new restaurants. Still, Marty wouldn't budge. He refused to serve meat.

Stanley had an idea. "Why don't you invite a food critic to come and review the food?" he suggested. "Most people don't know much about vegetarian food, but if it gets a good review, they'll all jump on the bandwagon!"

"That's a great idea," Marty agreed. He called the local newspaper and invited food critic Vernon Trey to visit Iceberg Islands.

As Marty was escorting Vernon to the Shamburger hut, Pat the cook was sizzling some Shamburgers on the grill.

"Hey, Dot," Pat called to her assistant. "Can you bring that bucket of barbecue sauce over to the counter? I'm trying out a new recipe for Tofu-lo Wings."

As Dot carried the bucket of sauce past the grill, she tripped over her own feet. The sauce splashed all over the burgers.

"Oh no!" Pat wailed. "Mr. Marty will be here any second."

And he was. Marty showed up at the Shamburger hut with Vernon. In a panic, Pat plopped a barbecue sauce-drenched burger on a bun and handed it to the food critic.

Vernon lifted the burger to his face, sniffed it, and then took a bite.

. . . .

Vernon chewed, swallowed—and was silent. Marty held his breath. What would Vernon's verdict be?

The food critic broke into a big grin. "Marty, this burger is *soy* delicious! I can't wait to try the other food in the park."

While Vernon munched on his burger, Pat pulled Marty aside. She told him all about the spilled sauce.

"Well, Vernon likes it. Let's put it on everything today," Marty suggested.

So Pat doused every burger and hot dog in the park with her barbecue sauce. She even added it to the pizza sauce.

It worked! For the first time, people were asking for seconds. And when Vernon's review came out a week later, it ended with, "A daringly original menu that digests so quickly, you'll never get sick—even on the Abominable Snow Coaster!"

Soon people were flocking to the park not only for the great rides, but for the healthy, unusual foods. Marty promoted Pat to head chef, and she created even more meatless dishes: baby-back "fibs," fake-and-bake chicken, and *barbecued* tofu on a stick.

"I guess if you slap down enough barbecue

sauce," Stanley said, munching on a barbecued pretzel, "anything's edible!"

"Now that the park is making money again, I'd like to create a whole new theme area," Marty said. "I was thinking of a medieval theme."

"Are you sure you want to introduce a new theme?" Stanley asked. "People seem to like this whole winter-wonderland thing. Maybe you shouldn't mess with it."

- **If Marty decides to stick with his theme and add more snowy attractions, go to page 52.**

- **If Marty decides to give his medieval idea a try, go to page 65.**

14 • • • •

"I think you're right, Sparky," Megnolia admitted. "Trying to build so many rides would totally wipe out my budget. Advertising might be the way to go."

The next morning, Megnolia walked downtown to meet with an advertising agency about her ad campaign. Suddenly, she heard the sound of wheels behind her. It was her friend Kenny, zipping down the sidewalk on his inline skates.

"Hey, Megnolia!" he said, skidding to a stop. "Where've you been?"

"Working on the theme park," she said, feeling a little guilty. Kenny was her best friend, and she had barely spoken to him since she got Big Bonnie's check.

"I'm on my way to an advertising meeting," Megnolia continued. "Opening day is coming soon!"

"What do you need advertising for when you've got me?" Kenny asked.

"What do you mean?" said Mcgnolia.

Kenny pointed down to his skates. "If you make up some fliers, I'll put them up all over town for you. It'll be quick, easy, and cheap!"

Megnolia thought about it. Kenny had a point. The ad agency wanted to do a big TV blitz that was costing Meg a fortune. Kenny's way would be much cheaper, and she'd be able to get her best friend involved in the park.

"It's a deal!" she said, smiling.

Megnolia had fliers printed up and delivered to Kenny. Then she concentrated on making a few last improvements to the park. With all the money she was saving, she could afford to build *two* coasters. She added a fast and furious hyper-coaster she named Bonnie's Comet. Then she built a small launched coaster with six inversions, so riders would spend most of the ride upside-down with their feet in the air!

Finally, opening day arrived. Kenny joined Megnolia at the front gate to watch people arrive.

The gates opened at 10 A.M. No one came. Megnolia started to sweat a little.

But at 12:47 people started arriving, and by 2 P.M. all the rides were full. Megnolia felt relieved, except for one thing: All of the guests in the park were wearing tights and colorful makeup. They also seemed to speak unusually loudly. The few people in the park who were not dressed up were chasing those who were, asking for autographs.

"Uh, Kenny, exactly where did you put up those posters?" Megnolia asked.

"Well, I put them in the places where I usually

skate," Kenny said. "Near the wrestling arena, at the Wrestler Dresser clothing store, and the Body Slam."

"The *what*?"

"The Body Slam. It's a restaurant where you eat great food and get to watch wrestling matches on giant TV screens," Kenny explained.

"Didn't you put them anywhere else?" Megnolia asked.

Kenny scratched his head. "Nope. That was it."

Suddenly the tights and makeup made sense. Megnolia took a deep, calming breath. "Do you mean to tell me," she said slowly, "that no one else knows about this park—except *wrestlers*?"

"I guess so. Isn't it great, though?" Kenny was thrilled. "I just saw Star Crunch talking to The Incredible Mister Mean!"

Megnolia was about to give Kenny a piece of her mind when the sound of shouting near the carousel caught her attention. She ran toward the noise, and Kenny followed.

A muscular man wearing a brown leotard was bellowing at the top of his voice. "Look out, Grim Reaper! The Dreadful Dog has his eyes on you! If you don't leave Crater Lake now, I'm going to drop you off the Silly Slide!"

. . . .

The crowd roared.

"Can't you read? There are no dogs allowed in this park, Dreadful!" shouted another very tall man, who Megnolia guessed was the Grim Reaper. "I'm going to send you back to the doghouse where you belong!"

The Dreadful Dog was outraged. He picked up the Grim Reaper with his powerful arms and hurled him into a nearby hot-dog stand. Buns and mustard splattered the walkway.

"They're going to ruin my park!" Megnolia screamed. Kenny just smiled, enjoying the show. Obviously, he wasn't going to be any help.

Megnolia had to think fast. She could call the police and have them clear out the wrestlers, but the bad press from that could ruin her park.

Megnolia popped a piece of gum in her mouth and chewed furiously. As she paced back and forth, Megnolia saw one of the wrestlers giving an autograph to a fan. The little boy gave the wrestler a hug and skipped back to his parents, beaming.

Hmmm. People really did seem to love the wrestlers. Maybe she shouldn't call the police after all. Maybe she should work *with* them instead. If she could keep the wrestlers happy, they'd really bring in the crowds!

- If Megnolia calls in the police, go to page 83.
- If Megnolia decides to work with the wrestlers, go to page 34.

. . . .

"You're right, Stanley," Marty said. "A Battle of the Bands would definitely get us a lot of publicity. Let's do it!"

Since Marty and Stanley had been so busy building roller coasters during the last few months, they hadn't paid much attention to the music scene. Marty picked up a copy of *Loud and Fast*, the leading rock music magazine, and made a list of the top bands in the country. Then he started making calls.

Luckily, being a roller coaster tycoon has its perks—one of them being that when you call the manager of a famous band, he'll actually take your call. First Marty called the manager of the Sappy Shins.

"Battle of the bands? I like the sound of that," she said. "We'll show the world that Sappy Shins rocks more than any other band!"

"Uh, great," Marty said. Then he tried the manager of Shredded Pork.

"Are the Sappy Shins playing?" the manager asked. "We won't do it if the Sappy Shins are playing."

"Uh, I don't think so," Marty lied. "Why, would that be a problem?"

"The Sappy Shins are always a problem," the

manager growled. "But don't worry. If they show up, we will show them that Shredded Pork rocks more than any other band!"

With the Sappy Shins and Shredded Pork on board, lining up other bands was easy. The battle grew into a three-day event, and thirty bands were signed up, including Shorty and John, Papercut, and the Porcelain Thrones.

The first day of the battle finally arrived. The park was filled to capacity by 10:30 A.M. The Sappy Shins took the stage at 11:00. And the trouble started at 11:31.

Marty had a hunch that his perfect day was about to be ruined when he saw his sister approach him backstage. She had a big grin on her face.

"Marty, are you crazy?" she asked him.

"What do you mean, crazy? The park is packed," he replied.

Megnolia shook her head. "No, I mean this lineup. Have you been living under a rock? These bands hate each other."

Marty began to sweat just a little. "What do you mean?"

Megnolia pointed to the guys in Shredded Pork, who were making their way to the stage area.

. . . . • • • • •

"Those guys *hate* the Sappy Shins. And those tattooed girls over there, the ones from Papercut, they all used to date Shredded Pork, but now they're not speaking."

Then Megnolia pointed to the Porcelain Thrones, who were waiting to take the stage next. "Plumber from the Porcelain Thrones used to be the drummer for Shorty and John, but they kicked him out. And…"

"Okay, okay, I get it," Marty said, trying not to panic. "But they're all mature human beings. Everything's going fine so—"

"*What are the Sappy Shins doing here*?" a loud voice bellowed.

Marty turned around to see the guitar player for Shredded Pork storming the stage.

"You stole the music to our song 'Greasy Spoon'!" he was yelling.

"Leave them alone!" one of the tattooed Papercut girls shouted. "You guys are a bunch of jerks!"

"Wait!" Marty cried, but his voice could not be heard above the angry, screaming rock stars. Papercut raced onstage and started pounding Shredded Pork with their drumsticks. Then the Porcelain Thrones and Shorty and John joined the fight. Soon the stage was a mess of flying guitar picks and snapping E strings.

"Please! I'm sure we can work something out!" Marty cried, but it was no use. Members of the other twenty-five bands rushed the stage, and security couldn't hold them back. The battle spread past the cable cars, around the new Sea Lion, and throughout the food courts. Soon the food was flying.

"What do we do now?" Marty asked Stanley.

"Run!" Stanley yelled.

Megnolia followed Marty and Stanley as they dodged flying Not Dogs and barbecued tofu. Thousands of park visitors ran with them.

Soon they arrived at the front gate. Marty waited until every barbecue sauce-coated guest had made it out safely. Then he locked the gate, containing all of the bands inside.

"When do you think they'll be finished?" Marty wondered.

"Probably not until everything in the park is destroyed," Stanley said sadly.

Megnolia put an arm around each of them. "Tell you what," she said. "I don't think your park is going to recover from this. Why don't you come work for me?"

· · · · · · · · ·

"Doing what?" Marty asked glumly. "Mowing the grass?"

"Look, Marty," Megnolia said. "I know we've had our differences. But you and Stanley are amazing coaster designers. I could use some more intense rides in my park. You can design all the rides you want. Just leave the publicity spectacles to me, all right?"

Marty and Stanley looked at each other. From inside the park, the sound of collapsing coasters made Marty cringe. Stanley nodded.

"We'll do it!" they said together.

THE END

Megnolia went straight to her office at Crater Lake. "Those bunnies were cute, but Mr. Fly is really cool," she said.

She contacted the comic book company and sealed the deal. They sent her dozens of Mr. Fly comic books to read. Megnolia couldn't get enough of them. She learned that when Mr. Fly was in his human form, he was a suave guy who wore bell-bottom pants and a polyester shirt. His arch rival was Henry Swat, a big-time crime boss who held the city in a grip of fear.

Megnolia loved the Mr. Fly concept so much that she changed the theme of Crater Lake. First, she renamed the park The Fly Trap. The Scare in the Air coaster became Fly in the Sky. The souvenir stands sold Mr. Fly action figures and T-shirts. The food stands featured Swat Dogs and Fly Burgers instead of hot dogs and hamburgers. (She did, however, pass on the maggot ice cream.)

Megnolia hit the jackpot! When the Mr. Fly movie opened, it was a huge success and attendance exploded. Megnolia was able to buy more land around The Fly Trap to expand the park. Soon the park doubled in size, and the number of coasters doubled, too.

From then on, it was smooth sailing for

Megnolia Butterfield and the park formerly known as Crater Lake. Big Bonnie couldn't have been more proud!

THE END

. . . .

"Kid! I love the idea! *Night of the Living Roller Coaster!*" Ray Ray told Stanley, who suddenly stood a little taller after having his idea praised by the famous director. "A theme park is a great setting for a horror movie. I can always do a musical next time."

The three sat around a table and brainstormed ideas for the movie.

"I like what Stanley said about evil aliens," Marty said. "We could have all of the ride operators brainwashed by aliens from Pluto. It's cold on Pluto like it is at Iceberg Islands, and that's what could attract them to the park."

"All the rides go crazy and start running at twice the usual speed," Stanley added through a mouthful of pretzels.

Ray Ray pounded his hands on the table. "The rides end up being a portal to Pluto. The Plutonians are kidnapping humans!"

Marty thought it sounded like the best idea for a movie he had ever heard. The film was shot in two months and became a huge hit. It scared millions of movie fans the first year it was out.

"The movie is a success," Marty told Stanley. "Fans of the film should start flocking to the park any day now."

But that day never came. Ray Ray Pettaway was such a horror-movie genius that the movie actually made people too terrified to set foot in Iceberg Islands. They were afraid of being kidnapped by Plutonians.

The DVD version of the movie was coming out next, which meant the legend of Iceberg Islands would never die. Marty had no choice but to close the park.

On the bright side, Marty and Stanley had made a deal to get part of the profits from the film, so they had more than enough money to start a new park. They thought about it, but in the end they were too busy working with Ray Ray on the latest installment in his *Camp Fear* series—*Screamsong: The Musical.*

THE END

Megnolia Butterfield couldn't wait to get started on her theme park. She hopped on her bike and rode down to the site she had in mind for Crater Lake.

What a site! It was a beautiful, flat area, but it wouldn't be flat for long. Magnolia took a notebook out of her pocket and began to sketch plans for the park grounds.

Everything took shape quickly. She hired a small staff, set up a trailer on the site to use as an office, and then started building. She dug a shallow hole on the lot and lined it with black craggy rocks. It looked just like a mctcor crash site! Then she filled it with water and planted unusual plants and flowers all around the lakc. With its mix of black rock and funky plants, the park already seemcd mysterious!

Next, she started building rides. She started with the basics: a carousel called The Orbit and a train to transport people around the park. She added a classic ride in which riders were whizzed around in saucer-shaped cars and called it Flying Saucers. And, of course, she added a roller coaster—a small wooden one she named Spaced Out. The coaster was only fifty feet high and topped off at forty-six miles per hour, but she was proud of it. It was a good start.

Finally, Megnolia hired a crew of mechanics to repair the rides and groundskeepers to water the garden and mow the grass. The park was ready to open, and there was plenty of time before coaster season started.

The more Megnolia thought about opening day, the more she got the jitters.

"We're a small park," she told her staff during a meeting. "My brother's Iceberg Islands is going to be opening the same time we are. I want to make sure we can compete!"

Megnolia's staff stared at her blankly. To tell the truth, they weren't much of a staff. There was Sparky, the head mechanic. Next to him was Clarence, the head groundskeeper. And then there was Lucy, who had just graduated with an engineering degree and would do anything to work on a theme park—even if it meant working for peanuts for Megnolia.

Finally, Lucy started waving her hand excitedly. "Why not fill Crater Lake with more rides than any other park in the country?" she suggested. "Your brother will never be able to compete with that."

Megnolia leaned back. "I like the sound of that. It would use up the rest of my money, though."

· · · · · · · · ·

Sparky shook his head. "My mechanics need to get the hang of taking care of the rides we have before we go ahead and add more. You've already got a nice place here. Why not spend some money on an advertising campaign? If you can get people through the gates, they'll like it, and they'll come back. And *then* you can build more rides."

- **If Megnolia splurges and builds tons of rides, turn to page 106.**

- **If Megnolia tries advertising the park, turn to page 15.**

・ ・ ・ ・ ・ ・ ・ ・

"Well, since you put it that way," Marty gave in. "Everyone should be able to enjoy my rides without any hassle. It's not your fault you're a superstar!"

August's puppy-dog expression vanished instantly, and he was all smiles again. "Thanks, Marty. You're the best!"

They chose a date for August to rent the park. All of Marty's staff, including Stanley, anxiously waited for that day.

When the day finally arrived, Marty was honored that he and Stanley were included on August's guest list.

"Are you kidding? I owe you guys big-time," August said, giddy with excitement. "I can't wait to go on all the rides!"

They started by riding the Joust—three times in a row, no waiting! August was loving every minute of it. By the end of the day, they must have ridden each ride at least eight times. Marty was surprised that a superstar could be such a fun, normal guy. August seemed to like Marty a lot, too.

"You know, Marty, you've got a lot of charisma," August said between bites of Tofuroni Pizza. They were all eating dinner in the medieval castle. "I have a lot of contacts in Hollywood. You could star in your own TV show!"

• • • • • • • • •

Stanley almost choked on his pretzel. Marty blushed.

"Me? On TV? No way," Marty replied.

"I'm serious," August said. "You'd be great. Stanley can take care of the park for a little while, can't he?"

Marty had to admit that the offer was tempting. Who wouldn't want to be a TV star? Then again, lots of people wanted to be roller coaster tycoons, too. Could he give that up—even for a little while?

- **If Marty decides to star in his own TV show, go to page 43.**
- **If Marty turns down the offer, go to page 70.**

Megnolia didn't want to have to call in the police on her opening day. She decided to try working things out with the wrestlers.

As she walked up to the two grappling giants, a short, stocky man with platinum blond hair stepped between them.

"Break it up, boys!" he barked. "This is a theme park, not a wrestling arena."

"It's Star Crunch!" Kenny said breathlessly. "When Star Crunch talks, everybody listens!"

Sure enough, the Dreadful Dog and Grim Reaper ended their fight. Megnolia walked up and shook Star Crunch's hand.

"Thank you, Mr. Crunch," she said. "I'm Megnolia Butterfield, the owner of Crater Lake."

"Nice to meet you, Meggie," he said. "You've got a great park here."

Megnolia cringed, but she didn't have the guts to tell the burly wrestler not to shorten her name. Besides, he seemed kind of nice.

"Thanks," she replied. "Listen, I was thinking. So far, you wrestlers have been my best customers. I'd love for you to come to my next staff meeting. You could help me think up ideas for the park that wrestlers would like."

Star Crunch beamed. "We could tag-team!"

Sparky, Lucy, and Clarence stared, open-mouthed, when Star Crunch arrived at the next meeting. He had come with a list of ideas.

Unfortunately, Megnolia had to shoot down most of them.

"Bumper cars without the bumpers?" Star Crunch asked.

"Too dangerous."

"Free wrestling boots to every park visitor?"

"Too expensive."

Finally, Star Crunch made a workable suggestion.

"How about a super-scary haunted house?" he said.

Megnolia thought about it. Haunted houses could be fairly easy to build, and they were fun. Then again, she'd read in *Coasters Illustrated* that visitors got tired of them pretty quickly.

"Let me think about it," she told Star Crunch.

- If Megnolia decides to build the haunted house, go to page 112.

- If Megnolia decides not to take any of Star Crunch's suggestions, go to page 38.

Marty decided to spend wisely.

"It's a good idea not to spend all of your money at once," Stanley admitted, pretzel crumbs flying out of his mouth. "Plus, little kids will *love* having a park created just for them. They'll come back with their families again and again! We'll be raking in the cash!"

So Marty built a fun and safe bumper-cars ride. Then he added a colorful spiral slide. Kids could climb to the top of a not-too-tall tower and slide down into a springy foam pad. He installed a boat ride for the lake, and built a hedge maze on one of the icebergs. Kids could walk through the maze, hitting dead ends if they made a wrong turn. But Marty made sure it wasn't too hard to find the exit.

Marty felt great about adding so many new rides for the same cost as one more coaster. He and Stanley walked proudly through the park. As they walked, they heard people's conversations.

"I want to go on something more exciting than the Spiral Slide!"

"Yeah, this park is lame!"

"There's another park downtown called Crater Lake. It has colossal coasters. Let's go there!"

Marty heard the sound of a stampede behind him. He and Stanley turned around to find a

. . . .

crowd of parents, children, and other park visitors rushing toward them.

"We want out!" shouted a crowd of grand-mothers.

"This place is for babies!" said a three-year-old.

"Hey everyone!" someone announced on a bullhorn. "Megnolia Butterfield is offering half-price admission to Crater Lake with a ticket stub from this dump!"

The entire crowd left—and never came back. One nice woman did return the next day, but she only wanted the umbrella she had left behind in the hedge maze.

THE END

· · · · · · · · ·

"Listen, Star Crunch," Megnolia said. "I really appreciate your ideas. But they're just not working for me. Sorry."

Star Crunch stood up and pounded his fist on the table. "Nobody insults Star Crunch!" he bellowed. Then he stormed out of the room.

"I thought you were very polite," said Sparky.

"Thanks, Sparky," Megnolia said. "I just hope this doesn't cause any trouble."

But the next morning, Megnolia found herself up to her neck in trouble. Star Crunch and the wrestlers were wreaking havoc inside the park. Some of the wrestlers were carrying signs that read MEGNOLIA BUTTERFIELD UNFAIR TO WRESTLERS. Others were expressing their feelings in a more physical way. Tigress was pile-driving Cat Girl into a pile of hot dog buns. Dreadful Dog was sitting on top of the Silly Slide, making it impossible for any kids to get past him. And a news crew was getting it all on camera.

Megnolia was furious. She'd done everything she could to keep the wrestlers happy and now they were ruining her park!

"That's it!" Megnolia screamed. "I've had it. Kenny, your tag-team pals have got to go!"

"Come on, Megnolia," Kenny said soothingly.

"We can still make this work. Their ideas aren't so great, but maybe we could hire them to operate the rides or something. They might like that, and the fans will love it. Everybody wins!"

Kenny hated the thought of kicking the wrestlers out. Plus, he was a little afraid of making them any angrier than they already were.

But Megnolia wasn't having it. "*Or*, we can just boot them out of the park for good, like I said," she said threateningly. Then she sighed. "But I can't just throw them out in front of the news crew."

Then she got an idea. "But maybe there *is* another way...."

- If Megnolia hires the wrestlers to work in her park, go to page 73.
- If Megnolia hatches a plan to get rid of the wrestlers once and for all, go to page 117.

Megnolia didn't think there was any way she and Marty could make a partnership work.

"Sorry, Marty," she said. "I'll have to turn you down."

But not long after that, Megnolia wondered if she had made the right decision. The puke-pouch gimmick was fading, just as she had guessed. She needed to find some way to generate interest in the park again.

"Any ideas?"

"How about a promotion?" Lucy suggested. "We could offer half-price admission to people who bring soda cans."

"Boring!" Star Crunch barked. "Most parks do that already. We need something with more punch!"

"This sounds like a job for the wrestlers," Megnolia said. "If anyone has punch, it's them."

Megnolia polled the wrestlers, and their ideas weren't all that bad. Tigress thought people should come to the park dressed as their favorite wrestler. The Grim Reaper suggested having people demonstrate a wrestling move to get half-priced admission.

But the idea Megnolia liked best came from Dreadful Dog.

"Chihuahuas," he said.

"Huh?" Megnolia asked.

"I have six of them at home," Dreadful said. "They're the most popular pet this year. Give reduced admission to people who bring their chihuahuas to the park."

"I love it!" Megnolia said. "They're so tiny, they won't cause any trouble."

Megnolia's chihuahua promotion began the very next week. On the first day, eight thousand people brought their chihuahuas to the park.

It only took about five minutes before Megnolia realized her mistake. Soon, the sound of eight thousand yapping chihuahuas filled the park. The screeching sounded like guitar feedback.

Megnolia also hadn't counted on how hungry chihuahuas could get. The park ran out of hamburgers and hot dogs before lunch!

That's about when Lucy came into her office.

"Uh, Megnolia," she said. "You know when I talked about giving discounts for soda cans? Well, usually the soda manufacturers give the park money for promotions like that," she said. "Who's going to reimburse you for the chihuahuas—chihuahua manufacturers?"

Megnolia groaned and rested her head on her

desk. Lucy was right. People were getting in for half price, but the park wasn't getting any money in return. They were losing money every minute a chihuahua entered the park!

Star Crunch burst into her office next.

"Come on, Meggie," he said. "We've got to get out of here!"

Star Crunch dragged her outside. To her horror, Megnolia saw that the park was overrun by yapping chihuahuas! Their owners couldn't control them anymore. There were simply too many chihuahuas in one place.

Megnolia, Star Crunch, and the rest of the staff managed to escape safely. Unfortunately, Megnolia had to abandon the park. The dogs had taken over.

It took weeks to round up all the chihuahuas and clean up the park. But by then, the park had lost so much money that Megnolia couldn't afford to reopen anyway.

For the rest of her days, Megnolia couldn't bear the high-pitched sound of tiny dogs yapping. It was too painful a reminder of the great park that she'd saved from a pack of wild wrestlers, but lost in the end to a bunch of toy-sized chihuahuas.

THE END

Marty realized he'd be crazy to turn down a chance at superstardom. "I'll do it!" he said. "Stanley will be a great leader while I'm gone."

August smiled, pleased. "Great! I'll fly you out to L.A. tomorrow so we can finalize the details."

It all seemed like a dream come true to Marty. Within days, he was sitting in August's posh L.A. office, reading over the script for his very own sitcom. Marty was to play a character named Marty who owned a theme park. (It wasn't much of a stretch.) The show focused on the wacky behind-the-scenes action of the park. He had a clumsy assistant who ate pretzels constantly, a younger sister who always wanted to be a step ahead of Marty, and enormous business troubles. August would guest star as himself, a roller coaster fanatic.

The network advertised the new show for weeks before the first episode aired. Marty was dragged onto every talk show on network TV. Soon the whole world knew the name Marty Butterfield.

"Things are great," Stanley reported during one of their daily phone calls. "Attendance at the park is at an all-time high. People want to see where Marty Butterfield really works!"

All the attention was giving Marty a lot of

confidence. He was sure the show was going to be a big hit.

Finally, the first show aired. In his hotel room, Marty watched the show and laughed at every joke.

He was the only one. The other two million viewers of the show sat in their living rooms, deadpan. No one laughed. Across the country, people agreed it was the worst show they had ever seen.

Poor Marty had no idea. The next day, he called Stanley to see what he thought of the show and to find out how things were at the park.

"Marty, we've been open for two hours now and no one is here."

"What?" Marty was shocked.

"Well, there *is* a small crowd outside the gate," Stanley said.

"Then let them in!" Marty said.

"They've got signs. They say, MARTY STINKS and MARTY'S A DUMMY! I'm sorry, Chief," Stanley said sadly.

"How could they turn on me so quickly?" Marty asked in disbelief.

"It gets worse, Chief."

"Worse than 'Marty Stinks'?"

"They're outside Crater Lake, too. Megnolia has just sold her park. She and your folks are loading a

· · · · · · · · ·

moving van. They're getting out of town and changing their names," Stanley explained.

Marty followed his family's lead. He currently sells shoestrings in Peoria, Illinois, and goes by the name Newell Nope.

THE END

Megnolia liked Clarence's suggestion. She'd always loved meeting costumed characters when she was a kid. It was something her park was definitely missing.

"But I'm not going to get just any dumb character," she said. "I'm going to buy the rights to the most popular cartoon character around!"

Unfortunately, Megnolia wasn't sure exactly who that was. To find out, she started reading stacks of comic books. She read about the Killer Bee, a super hero whose goal was to protect the environment from pollution. She read about Whale Man and his sidekick, Squid Kid, who kept watch over sailors and cruise ships. She read so many comic books she became cross-eyed.

None of the comic book characters seemed quite right for her park. Next, she tried watching all the TV cartoons she could stand, but none of them seemed right, either. Her eyes were starting to glaze over from watching so many shows. Megnolia decided to take a break.

She was out riding her bike when a movie poster caught her eye. Megnolia stopped.

The poster was for a film version of a new comic book character called Mr. Fly. According to the poster, Mr. Fly was a super-cool man-fly who fought crime using his ability to become a normal-looking housefly. He would sit as a fly on the wall and listen to the plans of the city's crime bosses. He nailed the bad guys every time.

"That's it!" Megnolia cried. She headed back home, her mind full of ideas. When she walked in the door, she heard Marty laughing. He was watching a TV show she had never seen before.

"What's this?" Megnolia asked.

"It's a new show called Fuzzy Bunnies. It's about a family of bunnies who run a grocery store, and at night…"

"They look so cute!" Megnolia interrupted. "Is it really funny?"

"Yes, it's *so* funny. You see, at night…"

Megnolia didn't stick around to hear the rest. She had a phone call to make!

- If Megnolia decides to feature Mr. Fly costume characters at the park, go to page 25.

- If Megnolia decides to feature the Fuzzy Bunnies characters instead, go to page 94.

• • • • • • • • •

"Are you kidding me? Call him back right now and tell him I'd love to collaborate!" Marty ordered Stanley.

They made the deal and a week later started working together. When Marty met MG for the first time, he had trouble speaking. "The...the Twevil In...I mean, the Evil Twin is my favorite ride, MG."

"Well, Frosted Pretzel is not so bad, either," MG replied. "I am looking forward to working on this new ride. I want to try something a little more... intense. In the first drop, the coaster will plunge down ninety feet and top off at seventy-four miles per hour. Then the riders will shoot directly into a triple loop. They'll experience a G-force of five point six. Ouch!"

Marty was horrified. He admired MG's desire to push the limits, but that was a little much. A G-force of 5.6 was like having more than five hundred pounds dropped in your lap!

"Um, that sounds great, MG," Marty began, wondering how to criticize the biggest roller coaster genius in the world. "I like the intensity, but maybe it's, um, *too* intense? The ride you're describing sounds pretty painful. No one would be able to ride it."

. . . .

MG looked thoughtful. "Perhaps you are right, Marty."

"We could bank the curves and raise the first loop after the drop," Marty suggested. "That would decrease the G-force, but the ride will still be awesome."

MG smiled. "I like it! Let's do it."

A few weeks later, the Abominable Snow Coaster was built, and it was a monster success. *Coasters Illustrated* ranked it as one of the top-ten coasters in the world! People came from all over the globe to ride the newest addition to Iceberg Islands.

"Can you believe all these people?" Marty asked Stanley.

The number of guests multiplied, and soon there weren't enough food stands to keep everyone fed. So far, Marty had only built popcorn stands and coffee shops.

"The next logical step for us, Chief, is to built a pretzel stand," Stanley suggested.

"We need more than just snack food," Marty said. "People want to fill up on real food like hot dogs, hamburgers, and pizza."

Stanley's stomach rumbled. He reached into his pocket for pretzels, but there were only crumbs and chunks of salt. He licked his fingers.

Marty continued. "But I've been a vegetarian for two years now. I'd feel funny serving meat in my park."

Stanley put his hand on his friend's shoulder. "Chief, people will never go for that. What'll you serve?"

"There are plenty of choices," Marty said, searching his mind for ideas. "Like…tofu on a stick! This could be my chance to get people to eat great vegetarian food. If they have no choice, they'll have to eat it."

"I think it's gross, Chief. And they do have a choice—they can leave the park."

- Should Marty stick to popular food such as hamburgers and hot dogs? If so, go to page 114.

- Or should he stick to his beliefs and sell only vegetarian food? If so, go to page 11.

. . . .

"I think Lucy's idea makes the most sense," Megnolia finally decided. "Let's give it a try."

Additional benches were installed near all the rides, and the puke level in the park went down to an acceptable level. That made Megnolia happy, but not the wrestlers. She found them gathered outside her office door one morning.

"Watching people puke was half the fun," Dreadful Dog said glumly.

"Yeah," agreed Tigress. "Now it's back to being boring."

"I guess what we're saying, Meggie," said Star Crunch, "is that we quit!"

Megnolia was relieved to see the wrestlers go, but attendance in the park dropped sharply. She called an emergency staff meeting.

"I think we should start advertising again," she began. "We've got to reach out to people who aren't wrestling fans."

Kenny raised his hand.

"Yes, Kenny?" Megnolia asked.

"I have an idea," he said. "I could skate around town and put up fliers...."

"*No, Kenny!*" said Megnolia, Sparky, Lucy, and Clarence.

THE END

"You've got a point, Stanley," Marty agreed. "I bet we can have fun thinking up more snowy stuff for the park."

Marty and Stanley munched on snow cones for inspiration. Once the brain freeze wore off, the ideas really started to flow.

"We can put fake snowmen along the paths," Marty said.

"What about trees with fake snow on them?" Stanley suggested. "We can line them up along the track of the Abominable Snow Coaster."

"How about a snow castle?" Marty added. "And a fake snow hill. People could go sledding in the middle of the summer!"

Using the profits from the food stands, Marty built all the new snowy attractions. He even hired professional ice skaters to put on shows, such as "Dinos on Ice."

This was Stanley's favorite. "You have not truly lived until you've seen a T-Rex do a triple axel," he liked to say.

Marty didn't stop there. He created T-shirts that read ICEBERG ISLANDS—SNOW PLACE LIKE HOME. He designed a water slide called Freezing Rain, and sold snow globes that boasted water made of actual melted snowballs from the North Pole.

Marty wasn't finished yet. "I want to try my hand at a hyper-coaster," he said, and went on to design a coaster even bigger and faster than the Abominable Snow Coaster. His new coaster was more than two hundred feet tall with a top speed of ninety miles per hour. He built it entirely over water with water spouts shooting water into the air at the bottom of each drop. He called it the Sea Lion.

All the new stuff brought in more crowds, but not the hordes that Marty was expecting.

"We need to find a way to let people know how cool the park is now," he told Stanley. "Regular advertising isn't enough. We need to do something special."

Marty leafed through the latest issue of *Coasters Illustrated* for ideas. Stanley chomped on pretzels, lost in thought.

"What about a Battle of the Bands?" Stanley finally suggested. "The top rock groups in the country will play at an all-day festival in the park until one group is crowned 'Coolest Band.' "

"Not bad," Marty said. "People will come to hear their favorite music, and they'll stay for the rides. I like it." Then something in the magazine caught his eye.

"Check this out," Marty said, pointing to a small ad. "It says, 'Famous filmmaker seeks coaster park for location of newest film. Contact Ray Ray Pettaway at 555-SCREAMS.' "

"I don't know," Stanley said. "Shooting a movie here would draw attention to the park. But I still think a Battle of the Bands would get us more publicity quicker."

- If Marty decides to host a Battle of the Bands, go to page 20.

- If Marty decides to let Ray Ray Pettaway shoot a movie in his park, go to page 104.

. . . .

While Megnolia knew that beef jerky was pretty tasty, it was pretty salty, too. She'd have to open up a bunch of additional drink stands to keep her customers happy. In the end, she wouldn't be saving much money at all.

Instead, she ordered the Dale Peril Growth-Spurt Stunter.

"So you see, Clarence," she told her head groundskeeper, "I'll need to let your staff go. All you have to do is pour this stunter stuff on the lawn once a month, and the grass never needs to be mowed. I can even do it myself!"

Clarence looked devastated. "Whatever you think is best," he said. Then, in a lower voice he muttered, "Not that I would trust any of Dale Peril's products with a ten-foot rake."

"What's that supposed to mean?" Megnolia demanded, frowning. But Clarence had already walked away to go tell his workers the bad news.

Clarence's comment worried Megnolia a little, but she chalked it up to sour grapes. Once she started applying the Growth-Spurt Stunter, she found that it worked beautifully. Though she hated to see the mowers go, the money she saved on their salaries was enough to keep the park in business.

．　．　．　．　．　．　．　．　．

When Megnolia walked through the park one sunny day, she couldn't have been happier. The rides were filled with people. The smell of pizza and hot dogs filled the air. Her beautiful green lawn shone in the sunlight. And strands of human hair blew past her in the breeze....

"Human hair?" Megnolia did a double-take. The hair was flying off of Bonnie's Comet, one of the hyper-coasters. Megnolia watched as riders got off the ride. They were missing patches of hair!

Megnolia ran around the park in a panic. Everywhere she looked, park visitors were missing eyebrows, sideburns, and ponytails.

Clarence's warning about the Growth-Spurt Stunter echoed in her mind. She ran to the storage shed and picked up a container of the stunter. Then she read the fine print: "Prolonged exposure to Dale Peril Growth-Spurt Stunter may cause skin irritation." The finer print read: "That means it will make you bald—very bald."

Megnolia screamed and ran out of the shed. As she raced down the hairy walkway, she caught her reflection in the lake. She was completely bald except for a strip of hair down the center of her head.

"Oh, no!" she screamed in horror. "A mohawk!"

• • • • • • • • •

Megnolia went broke paying for wigs and hair-replacement treatment for every visitor to the park. Megnolia had to admit defeat and close Crater Lake.

On the bright side, she had just enough money left to buy a really nice hat until her mohawk grew out.

THE END

"A 3-D movie? That's genius!" Ray Ray said. "It's been too long since the world has seen a great 3-D movie, and we're going to give it to them— *Roller Coaster Pie Party.* I see it," he paused, "as a comedy!"

The boys encouraged Ray Ray's new idea. "What's the plot, Ray Ray?" Marty asked.

"Bart owns the amusement park, but he's a real crook. He cuts his employee's wages, waters down the soda in the food stands, and..." Ray Ray paused again. He looked at Stanley, and his eyes widened. "He cheats his partner and best friend out of his share of the park!"

"You're a genius, Mr. Pettaway," Stanley said. Marty could tell he liked the idea of a "business partner" starring in the movie.

"So where does the 3-D magic come in?" Marty piped up.

"Isn't it obvious? We'll have the rides fly right into the audience's faces. The cars on the suspended coaster will seem to fly right out of the screen!" Ray Ray rubbed his hands together and licked his lips. "And for the finale..." Ray Ray paused a third time, took a deep breath, and said, "a giant pie fight!"

His speech was so inspiring that Marty and

Stanley applauded. They couldn't wait for filming to begin.

A few days later, Ray Ray stopped by the park with more exciting news. "You'll never guess who's starring in the movie," Ray Ray said. "James Carryon!"

Marty couldn't believe it. James Carryon was the best comic actor in the business. The movie was going to be great!

But Marty couldn't help feeling a little twinge of guilt. Carryon was Megnolia's favorite actor. She would give anything to meet him. The trouble was, he and his sister hadn't even spoken since they had argued about what to do with Big Bonnie's money. Not easy to do, since they lived in the same house! But he had to admit he missed her—just a little bit.

One morning, Marty left Megnolia a note. "Meet me at Iceberg Islands today. Come early. Your brother, Marty." Even if she was still angry with him, Marty knew her curiosity would lead her to the park.

He was right. Megnolia walked through the park gates right after Marty arrived. Ray Ray's crew was setting up a table piled high with lemon meringue pies for the big pie fight.

Megnolia put her hands on her hips and frowned at Marty. "What's with the mysterious message? Did you want me to come see you fail in person?"

Marty didn't answer. He waited for Megnolia to notice James Carryon as he walked onto the set.

Megnolia's arms dropped to her sides. Her eyes grew wide.

"Is...is that...?" she stammered.

Marty nodded. "James Carryon. I thought you'd want to meet him."

"You thought? Of course I do! I'm his biggest fan!" Megnolia snapped, back to her old self. "James, I loved you in *Follow That Gopher*!"

Megnolia ran toward the actor. At the same time, Ray Ray Pettaway yelled, "Action!"

The pies began to fly. The first one hit Megnolia right in the face!

Megnolia stopped. Then she licked the meringue out of her mouth. "Marty, is this some kind of setup?" she yelled.

"Cut! Cut!" yelled Ray Ray.

Megnolia wasn't listening. She picked up a pie and hurled it right at Marty. He was too stunned to duck.

Splat! The gooey pie covered Marty's face.

Marty wanted to be angry, but he couldn't. There was just something funny about getting hit by a pie.

Marty grabbed a fresh pie and hurled it at Stanley. "Hey, partner!" he yelled.

Stanley caught it with his left hand, walked off, and ate it with his right.

"I said cut!" Ray Ray yelled again.

Megnolia threw another pie at Marty. Marty grabbed a pie in each hand and countered by smooshing one on Megnolia's face and the other on the back of her head.

"Two pies are better than one," Marty said, laughing.

Soon Megnolia was laughing, too. The siblings slid to the ground, giggling uncontrollably.

"I can't believe we've been mad at each other for so long," Megnolia said. "We used to have fun together."

"Maybe we can still have fun together," Marty said. "Our parks are pretty close to each other. We could merge them into one big park."

"The Butterfield Megapark," Megnolia said. "Big Bonnie would be proud."

From the sidelines, Stanley shook his head. "Only those two could make peace during a pie fight."

· · · · · · · · ·

A year later, Marty and Megnolia were still getting along. Their megapark was breaking attendance records, and *Roller Coaster Pie Party* was breaking records at the box office.

Ray Ray called Marty to talk about making *Roller Coaster Pie Party 2: À la Mode.*

THE END

"Star Crunch, this is not working out," she said, choosing her words carefully. "Let's face it. You and your friends were born to wrestle, not to operate rides. You're too good for this park!"

Star Crunch thought about that. "You know what, Meggie?" he replied. "You're right! Me and my wrestlers will clear out of here this afternoon. I'll miss you, Meggie."

Megnolia would miss Star Crunch, too, but it was nice to have the park back to normal. She hired new ride operators who were in an amusement park workers' union. They took the job seriously and worked for much less than the celebrity wrestlers.

Without the wrestlers bringing in the crowds, Megnolia had to think of another way to jazz up the park. She decided to build a new ride: an air-powered vertical coaster that topped off at eighty-five miles per hour. It rose two hundred feet in the air, then dropped straight down. Megnolia went on all the test rides and loved the rush she got when the coaster dropped. She called it the Scare in the Air. It was a huge hit.

But she still needed more ideas to draw in bigger crowds. She held another staff meeting—although it did feel a little lonely without Star Crunch.

"No more rides," said Sparky. "My crew and I are overworked as it is."

"I know, Sparky," Megnolia sighed. "Anyone else?"

"I've been doing some research," Lucy said. "No park in the country serves gourmet food. Why not hire a famous chef for the park?"

Megnolia liked the sound of that, but Clarence frowned and shook his head.

"Nobody cares about that fancy-schmancy stuff," he said. "What you need are people walking around in cute costumes—for the little kids, you know? Every park does it!"

Megnolia was stumped. Both ideas sounded great. But which one should she choose?

- **If Megnolia decides to hire a gourmet chef for the park, go to page 101.**

- **If Megnolia decides to hire costumed characters, go to page 46.**

"I think I've had enough snow for one lifetime," Marty finally decided. "A medieval theme is just the change I need."

So Marty began designing a medieval marketplace to add to Iceberg Islands. He built a small castle that visitors could explore. He designed all the food and souvenir stores to look like the colorful tents found in marketplaces long ago. He designed a river rapids ride that wound around a fake cliff. He even hired his old friend MG to work with him on a new suspended, looping coaster he called the Joust. The ride wasn't too fast, but it had lots of fun curves.

Marty was admiring the Joust one sunny afternoon when a brown wig fell from the ride and landed at his feet. Marty looked up. A man in one of the cars was frantically clutching at his head. The wig must have fallen off when his car went through the first loop.

When the ride ended, Marty approached the man. He wasn't bald, as Marty expected, but sported a head of golden blond hair. There was something familiar about him.

Suddenly, a woman squealed, "It's August Sterling! Oh my goodness!"

A crowd of people surged around the man

before Marty could get any closer. He couldn't believe what he had heard. August Sterling was a superstar! His movies were blockbusters, his television show was number one in the ratings, and he had just won a Grammy for his latest solo album.

"I have all your CDs!" a man was screaming.

"Please sign my elbow!" yelled an elderly woman.

It looked like August was about to be trampled. Marty knew he had to do something. He pushed his way through the crowd, grabbed August by the arm, pulled him into the ride operator's booth, and locked the door.

"Don't worry, Mr. Sterling," Marty said. "I'm Marty Butterfield, the park owner. I'll call security and we'll get you out of here safely."

"Thank you," August said, looking relieved. "I usually don't go out in public, but I just had to visit your park. I love roller coasters, and I especially love the medieval period. I couldn't resist the combination of the two."

"Thanks," Marty said, flattered.

"I disguised myself so I could go out without being hassled," August continued. "But I guess that didn't work. As far as I can figure, there's only one way for me to enjoy myself in your park."

"What's that?" Marty asked.

August smiled, flashing perfect white teeth. "Would you consider renting the park to me?" he asked. "You could close the park for a day, and I'll pay you what you normally make on a business day. I'd bring a few friends with me, and you'd keep your employees on duty so we can go on all the rides."

"I don't know," Marty said. "I'd love to do a favor for a coaster lover, but I'd hate to lock out my guests, even for a day. They've kept me in business all this time."

Now August's expression changed to the saddest puppy-dog face Marty had ever seen. "Please," August pleaded. "I don't get to do anything normal anymore without my fans attacking me. I mean, I love them, but a guy's gotta have some kind of life, right? Coasters are my passion. If you don't do this for me, I may never be able to ride a coaster again!"

- **If Marty decides to rent the park to August Sterling for a day, go to page 32.**
- **If Marty refuses to rent the park to August, go to page 81.**

. . . .

"Sorry, Count Von Vamp," Megnolia said. "I'm not looking to hire anyone new right now."

So Megnolia opened the haunted house without the Count. On the first day it opened, Star Crunch and his wrestlers waited anxiously on line.

"This is going to be awesome!" Star Crunch said.

"I hope so," said the Grim Reaper. "It'll take more than a bunch of stupid fake skeletons to scare me!"

Megnolia grinned. She and Kenny had worked hard to make the haunted house a super-scary experience. She knew the wrestlers would love it.

Megnolia watched the first group enter the house. Within seconds, the sounds of terrified screams ran through the park.

"We did it!" Megnolia said happily, giving Kenny a high five.

A few minutes later, the wrestlers piled out of the house, looking pale and shaking all over.

"Meggie, are you crazy?" Star Crunch asked. "That haunted house is insane!"

The Grim Reaper was actually crying. "Please, get me away from here. It's just too much!"

Megnolia watched in disbelief as the wrestlers rushed away. The rest of the people in line followed them, too afraid to go in.

The wrestlers and their fans never came back to the park. The haunted house, Megnolia's star attraction, was constantly empty. Word got around that it was too scary, even for wrestlers. She was losing money every day.

One day she got another call from Count Von Vamp. He had heard about her troubles, and offered to buy the park from her—cheap. Megnolia had no choice. She sold the park to the Count, who turned it into a successful horror theme park.

In the meantime, Megnolia got a job writing a column for *Coasters Illustrated* called "How *Not* to Run a Theme Park."

THE END

"I don't think so, August," Marty told his new friend. "It's pretty tempting, but the park is where I want to be. Just Stanley and me calling the shots and designing hot coasters."

"I guess it is pretty cool having your own personal playground," August said, sounding a little jealous.

Marty laughed. "Yeah, I'd hate to be so famous that I couldn't go out in public without a wig!"

August finished his pizza. "Well, thanks again for letting me rent the park, Marty," he said. "Today was awesome."

Marty shook his hand. "If you ever want another day at Iceberg Islands, just give me a call."

"Sounds nice, but I don't know how often I can afford the hefty price of a day's business," August said. "Maybe I could come back with a better disguise than a three-dollar wig and spirit gum."

August left the park, and things got back to normal for Marty and Stanley.

"You know, Medieval Market is great, but I think we could expand even more," Marty told Stanley one afternoon.

Stanley sighed. "Listen, Marty. I know that we've got to constantly improve the park if we're going to stay ahead of the competition. But it's like all we ever do anymore is work. I'm pretty burned out at this point."

Marty understood. "I know," he said. "Let's take the night off. Maybe watch a video or something."

So that night Marty and Stanley stuffed themselves with Chinese food ("No food from Iceberg Islands!" Stanley had said) and pretzels (or Stanley did, at least). They played some video games, and then Stanley popped a DVD into Marty's entertainment system.

"It's August Sterling's last movie," Stanley said. "We never had time to see it in the theaters."

The film was a musical called *Samurai Beach Party*. Marty and Stanley watched as their friend laughed, cried, sang, and danced his way across a tropical beach. The extras in the film screamed and cheered as he performed.

Marty got a dreamy look in his eyes. "Imagine what it would be like to have entertainment like that at our park? Too bad we can't hire someone like August Sterling for Iceberg Islands."

Stanley hit the pause button the remote control. "Earth to Marty? You're friends with August now, remember? Why not call him up?"

"Of course!" Marty said, reaching for the phone.

Stanley sank back into the couch. "One night off," he muttered. "All I wanted was one night off."

A month later, August Sterling was opening his new series of concerts inside Iceberg Islands. People came in droves to ride Marty's rides and to hear August rock. And at the end of each night, after the crowds had all gone home, August had the park all to himself.

THE END

"Just give them one more chance," Kenny begged. "Please?"

Finally, Megnolia gave in. "All right, all right. But only because they bring in so much business!"

Megnolia took a breath and walked up to Star Crunch.

"Star Crunch, I want you guys to be happy," she said. "What if I hired your guys to work in the park? They can run the rides and do a nightly wrestling show. What do you think?"

"Wow," said Star Crunch. "I thought you didn't want anything to do with us."

"Nah, I kind of like you," she replied. "I'd just like to keep my park in one piece!"

"We're on it," Star Crunch said firmly. "Don't worry, Meggie. We won't let you down."

Megnolia and Star Crunch worked out a plan. The wrestlers would appear in full costume to run the rides. Each wrestler got a three-hour break to ride the coasters. And they would all participate in the nightly wrestling match, the Crater Lake Crunch!

The crowds went wild for it. Attendance rose by 20 percent! Megnolia was able to add a Ferris wheel, go-carts, and a bike-on-a-track ride.

The park was expanding, and things were

working out great, but Megnolia's happiness didn't last long. A few weeks later, Megnolia saw a kid fly from the bottom of the Silly Slide and skid all the way across the garden.

That was pretty unusual, since the Silly Slide was such a gentle ride. Once you reached the bottom, you just sat there. She walked over to the slide to see what was wrong.

On the way, she overheard people talking.

"Whoa! I feel sick, and I've only ridden the carousel."

"I just puked on the go-carts!"

Megnolia stormed up to the Silly Slide and found Dreadful Dog running the ride. Kids were whizzing down the normally tame slide at lighting speed.

"Dreadful, did you do something to the slide?" she asked.

Dreadful Dog beamed proudly. "Grease!" he said. "Lots of it. This ride used to be for wimps, but now it rocks!"

Megnolia groaned and made her way to the other small rides in a panic. Just as she suspected, the wrestlers were causing trouble all over the park. The Tenderizer had added potholes to the go-cart racetrack, Pam the Ram had doubled the speed of the Ferris wheel, and the Jelly Monster had removed the handlebars from the bike-on-a-track ride. Thanks to the hyped-up rides, the park walkways were covered with vomit.

A scream was building up inside Megnolia. She was almost ready to fire every last wrestler when she heard her customers raving.

"Crater Lake is the best. Who cares if I puked? I'm having so much fun!"

"Ferris wheels are usually lame, but not at Crater Lake!"

Megnolia couldn't believe it. People were happy about the souped-up rides! Word got around, and soon the park was more crowded than ever before.

The only problem was the puke.

"Megnolia, my handymen can deal with a little barf," Clarence told her at the next staff meeting, "but this is getting out of control. Can you please do something?"

"Why not add benches outside the rides?" Lucy suggested. "That way riders can rest between rides. They won't feel as nauseous."

"You need something flashier than that," said Star Crunch. "Why not sell Official Crater Lake Puke Pouches? Then people can catch their own barf!"

Megnolia liked both ideas, but there was another one she was afraid to say in front of Star Crunch: She could fire the wrestlers and keep them out of her park once and for all!

- If Megnolia installs benches near the rides, go to page 51.

- If Megnolia sells Crater Lake Puke Pouches, go to page 9.

- If Megnolia fires the wrestlers, go to page 63.

Stanley's argument was very persuasive.

"You're right," Marty agreed finally. "I'm borrowing the full two million dollars. If we're going to stay on top of our game, we've got to built the new three-hundred-sixty degrees coaster right away."

Marty designed the new coaster, and construction started the day the bank approved his loan. The ride was finished just in time for the new season. Iceberg Islands was the first park in the region to have anything like it.

He called it Ice Cube, and it was a tremendous success. It made every top ten list, and got glowing reviews in all the major magazines. The guests loved the coaster and were even willing to stand in two-hour lines for a chance to ride it!

But there was one thing Marty didn't count on: the high cost of maintaining it. First, he was paying a very high rate of interest on the loan. Then he had to hire extra handymen to monitor the dizzying effects of the rotating cars. It was more than he could afford.

To cut costs, Marty fired many of the park's handymen. He kept the mechanics to make sure the rides were safe, but there was no one left to pick up garbage, clean the water in the lake, or scrub the bathrooms. Soon the park was so messy and smelly that the crowds got smaller and smaller. With less money coming in, Marty's loan payments were late for six months in a row.

Marty and Stanley hung out by the front gate one morning, wondering if any guests would show up that day. Marty brightened when a small sports car drove up.

A man got out of the car, walked up to the gate, and attached a padlock the size of a small car to the gate. Then he hung a red sign that said, CONDEMNED.

Stanley handed Marty his bag of pretzels. "Here, Chief," he said. "You look like you could use these."

Marty ignored Stanley. He shoved his hands in his pockets and started walking down the street.

"Where are you going?" Stanley called out.

"To see Megnolia at Crater Lake," Marty yelled back. "It looks like I need a job!"

THE END

Just thinking about the beef jerky made meat-loving Megnolia's mouth water. She dialed the 800 number and ordered twenty-five Dale Peril Jerky Makers.

The following week, she closed all the burger joints and pizza stands and fired almost all the food service employees. She replaced them with Make-Your-Own-Jerky Huts. She wasn't sure if the jerky tasted great or if her guests were so hungry they would eat anything, but they were gobbling up the salty dried meat faster than you could say "profits"!

Megnolia walked through the park, pleased with herself. It seemed that every man, woman, and child was chomping down on beef jerky. But soon she noticed a problem.

"This jerky is making me thirsty!" one visitor complained.

"Aren't there any drinks in this park?" another cried.

Just then, Megnolia's cell phone rang. It was Kathy Baker, the park's food service manager. She was frantic.

"Today's drink shipment hasn't arrived and people are—"

"I know, I know." Megnolia cut her off and hung up the phone.

She groaned as a little boy yelled, "This jerky is

for jerks!" and threw his jerky into the lake. As Megnolia watched in horror, more park guests followed the lead of the jerky-throwing little boy. Soon Crater Lake was filled to the brim with discarded beef jerky!

"Uh, free tickets for everyone!" Megnolia yelled, but it was too late. Disgusted park guests were streaming out of the park. To make matters worse, the jerky was soaking up all the water in the lake. It looked like an old-fashioned tar pit!

Megnolia called an emergency staff meeting.

"So, Clarence," she said. "Do you think you and the grounds crew can clean up our lake?"

Clarence slid a piece of paper across the table. It was filled with numbers. "That'll cost you overtime," he said.

Megnolia looked at the numbers. Then she looked at her budget. It was not going to happen.

"Well, gang," she said. "Looks like this will be the end of Crater Lake."

"Oh, Megnolia," said Lucy. "What will you do now?"

Megnolia shook her head.

"I don't know," she said glumly. "But maybe I should get into the infomercial business!"

THE END

"I can't do it," Marty decided. "My park guests are too important to me."

August pleaded and offered even more money. Marty felt bad that August couldn't enjoy the park because of his celebrity status, but he stood firm. August shook Marty's hand. "I understand," he said. "Thanks for saving me from that crowd."

"No problem," Marty said. He used the phone inside the booth to call a security team. They made sure August got out of the park safely.

Marty returned to his office to find his phone ringing. He picked up the receiver.

"*Hey*, Marty!" a voice screamed.

Marty flinched. It was Heidi, the head of his research-and-development team. The team was responsible for staying on top of the latest trends and discoveries in the world of coaster design.

"I just got off the phone with the aeronautics team," Heidi said, still yelling. She was always excited about something. "There's a new way to build a coaster that has the riders' seats on the *outside* of the track. This allows the rider to rotate three hundred sixty degrees, independently from the train! One is already being built in the South, but there aren't any in our region. If we get one built for next season, we'll be the only park around here with this new type of ride!"

Marty loved the idea. "I'll check the coaster budget," he said. "If we have money to develop this, we'll do it!"

It didn't take very long for Marty to learn that he didn't have enough for pay for the new coaster. Once again, he and Stanley were picking each other's brains for ways to make money for the park.

"Well, Chief, we could borrow the money," Stanley suggested.

Marty frowned. He hadn't had to take out any loans so far, and he didn't want to start getting into debt now.

"If we borrow two million dollars, we could have the ride this season. We should be able to pay it off within two seasons," Stanley proposed. He really wanted to see this ride built.

"Maybe we could just borrow five hundred thousand dollars," Marty said. "We could use that to build a smaller ride this season. That would increase attendance and bring in more cash. Then we'd have enough to build the big ride."

- **If Marty borrows $500,000 and builds a smaller ride first, go to page 110.**

- **If Marty borrows $2 million and builds the new coaster, go to page 77.**

Megnolia called the police, and she was glad she did. By the time they arrived, every wrestler in the park was involved in a mega-battle. They crushed her beautiful plants, dented her rides, and demolished her food stands.

She was surprised and relieved when the wrestlers left the park peacefully. And it looked like she was in the clear—not one reporter showed up!

That night, Kenny called her on the phone.

"Megnolia, turn on Channel Seventeen right now!" he said urgently.

Megnolia turned on the television to Channel 17, the Wrestling Channel. The Dreadful Dog was standing in the ring, shouting into the microphone.

"Megnolia Butterfield, you are a spineless coward!" he yelled. "You called in the police to do your dirty work for you. Why don't you come challenge the Dreadful Dog face-to-face!"

Anger rose up in Megnolia like a thunderstorm. "Maybe I will!" she yelled back to the television.

Megnolia hurried downtown to the wrestling arena. The security guards seemed to know who she was. They let her right backstage.

Megnolia ran into the ring. The Dreadful Dog had his back to her. She grabbed a plastic folding chair that was propped up in the corner, then tapped him on his muscular shoulder.

"How's this for face-to-face, Dog?" she said. Then she whacked him over the head with the chair.

The Dreadful Dog collapsed in a heap. Megnolia took the microphone from his hands.

"Nobody messes with Megnolia Butterfield!" she roared into the mike. The crowd cheered. Megnolia pumped her fist into the air. The adrenaline rush was awesome!

Megnolia became an overnight wrestling sensation, and she loved it. The rush she got from being in the ring was even better than the excitement of riding an intense coaster.

Megnolia sold Crater Lake to Marty, who started hosting Wild Wrestling Wednesdays in the park. Every week Megnolia, her new manager Kenny, and all her wrestling friends could ride for free in exchange for performing matches in the park.

THE END

Ray Ray frowned again at the 3-D idea.

"On second thought, Ray Ray," Marty said, "I think you should go for the musical! You said it's been a lifelong dream. I wouldn't have this park if Big Bonnie hadn't encouraged me to follow my dream."

"Thank you, Marty!" Ray Ray replied. "You won't be disappointed."

One week later, Ray Ray came by and dropped a script on Marty's desk.

"I've been so inspired, Marty," Ray Ray said. "It's all thanks to you. Let me know what you think."

Marty leafed through the script while Stanley looked over his sholder and Ray Ray stared at them both with an anxious look on his face.

"It's the story of an orphan baby who was left outside the gates of a roller coaster park," Ray Ray explained excitedly as they were reading. "The boy is raised by a family of performing seals and survives by eating Not Dogs and Shamburgers. Wait'll you hear his show-stopping number: 'I'm Just a Lonely Rollercoaster Baby.' "

Ray Ray looked at Marty and Stanley expectantly.

"It sounds, uh…interesting," Marty said.

. . . .

"Just you wait," Ray Ray promised. "This is going to be my best movie ever!"

When Ray Ray left, Stanley cornered Marty. "Are you sure you want to do this? We have to close the park for two weeks so we can film here. This movie sounds like it's going to flop, big-time!"

"Ray Ray directed *The Claw* and *Dig My Grave*, two huge hits," Marty reminded him. "I trust him."

Shooting began a few weeks later. Marty lost money on admissions, but Ray Ray did hire the park to provide food for the cast and crew.

Marty sold Not Dogs and Lasoygna while Ray Ray's actors sang and danced their way around Iceberg Islands. He had to admit it looked like a lot of fun.

"Maybe you were right to trust Ray Ray after all," Stanley admitted. "That 'Rock Around the Roller Coaster' number was pretty exciting."

On the last day of shooting, Marty and Stanley walked into the park to find it filled with hundreds —maybe thousands—of tap dancers. Marty stared, dumbfounded, as Ray Ray pushed his way through the crowd toward him.

"It's the big finale," Ray Ray said, grinning. "One thousand and one tap dancers dancing on an iceberg. I'm going to shoot it from a helicopter. Wanna come?"

"It's gotta be safer up there than down here," Stanley whispered, motioning toward the hordes of dancing feet.

Marty and Stanley were hovering above the park in Ray Ray's helicopter when the director called "action!" The cameras were rolling. Down below, a thousand tap dancers began banging their feet on one of Marty's icebergs.

As the dancers danced, the iceberg began to rumble and creak. To Marty's horror, a crack appeared in the middle of the iceberg.

"Stop!" Marty yelled. "Those tap dancers are destroying the park!"

But he was too late. The sound of taps turned to screams as the iceberg broke in two. One thousand and one dancers, three major rides, and three thousand Not Dogs slid into the icy water.

Luckily, the rescue workers on set were able to get the situation under control. Marty's lake wasn't very deep, so no one was hurt badly—except for the park, of course. Marty was crushed.

Ray Ray, on the other hand, was thrilled.

"I got everything on film!" he said, beaming. "This is going to be bigger than the Titanic!"

And it was. *Singing in the Roller Coaster* became such a hit that people flocked to Iceberg Islands as soon as it was repaired. Marty and Stanley converted the park to a movie-theme park and, like the characters in the movie, they lived happily ever after.

THE END

. . . .

"That's a great idea!" Megnolia said. "I'd love for you to join the Crater Lake team!"

So when the haunted house opened, Count Von Vamp was stationed at the doorway, greeting guests and signing autographs. The line for the haunted house was longer than any other line in the park.

Count Von Vamp was working out so well that Megnolia hired some of his friends, too. There was Honey Helpless, a B-movie "Scream Queen" who had lent her shrieks to more than one hundred movies; Greg the Ghoul, from the old TV show; and several others.

The new park visitors loved it. Now Crater Lake was filled with guests—not just wrestlers, but true horror fans wearing black clothes, pale makeup, and spider jewelry.

Things were working out so well that Megnolia began plans to design some new, horror-themed rides. One day while she was breaking ground for a new Spider Coaster, Star Crunch and his wrestlers approached her.

"What happened to this park, Meggie?" Star Crunch asked.

"What do you mean?" she replied. "We're doing great business!"

The Dreadful Dog stepped forward. "But now the place is full of freaks! All the new visitors wear weird clothes."

"Yeah," added Star Crunch. "And funny make-up!"

Megnolia tried not to laugh. She couldn't believe that the wrestlers, of all people, were freaked out by the horror fans.

"Sorry Meggie," Star Crunch said. "We're just not comfortable here anymore."

Megnolia was sorry to see her friends go, but the park was doing such great business that she didn't have much time to mope. She turned Crater Lake into a horror theme park that ran successfully for many years.

THE END

After dealing with wrestlers all these months, Megnolia knew she'd be able to deal with Marty.

"Let's do it!" she told her brother.

"Great!" Marty said. "Stanley has helped me keep this place running. I'd like to keep him on board."

"That's fine, because I've been working with Star Crunch, the wrestling champion," Megan boasted. "He's got to be in on this, too."

"No problem," Marty said.

Agreeing with each other was easier than they thought. It didn't hurt that they doubled their money when they combined bank accounts. They built five new rides in the first year and a high-speed monorail connecting the two parks.

In honor of the lakes in their parks, they named their megapark Butterfield Lakes. The park continued to grow bigger and better with each passing season. Big Bonnie was so proud! Many years later, they passed the park on to their own great-grandchildren.

THE END

. . . .

After discussing it with Stanley, Marty finally decided to let MG do his magic.

"The man has more top-ten coasters than anyone in the world! I'll let him do it, and I'll just watch," Marty said.

They broke ground soon after their first meeting. Marty watched the coaster go up piece by piece and grew more and more anxious each day.

Finally, the ride opened. A red neon sign flashed the words FLAMING DEATH over the entrance. The track was painted blood red, and the cars resembled black coffins.

The crew took the first ride. Marty, Stanley, and MG sat in the first two cars of the train. Marty looked down. Below them was a steep ninety-foot drop. It looked pretty intense, even for Marty.

The train lurched forward as the ride operator released the brake. MG leaned over to Marty and Stanley and shouted, "Thanks for letting me go wild with this. *Good luuuuuuck!*"

The train plummeted down the first drop. Marty had never felt anything like it. His stomach was already doing somersaults and things only got more intense.

From the drop, they shot directly into a triple loop. Marty's brain rattled in his skull as the cars whizzed around the loops at an insane seventy-four miles per hour. The G-force at the top of the loop was phenomenal. Marty's whole body shook as the force slammed into him. His head felt as though it had detached from his neck.

When the train arrived back at the station, MG was laughing hysterically, but Marty and Stanley were as pale as the fake snow on the icebergs.

Every cell in Marty's body ached. His head was throbbing. Watching his crew stumble from the ride, clutching at their heads, Marty knew this ride was just too intense to let paying customers go anywhere near it. He had to shut down the ride before it even opened.

That didn't stop MG from sending him a bill, which cost Marty every bit of the rest of his money from Big Bonnie. To make things worse, without a cool ride like the Frosted Pretzel to draw people to the park, the crowds got smaller and smaller. Eventually, they stopped coming, and before long Marty was forced to sell the park and the land—to MG.

Today, Marty and Stanley can be found running the go-carts at Megnolia's park, Crater Lake.

THE END

"I want those Fuzzy Bunnies!" Megnolia cried as she headed straight for her office at Crater Lake.

She contacted the people at the Fuzzy Bunnies show and made a deal. They sent her a glossy style guide with the names and pictures of all the bunnies. They sent her some videotapes, too, but Megnolia didn't feel as though she needed to watch them. The bunnies were adorable—what else did she need to know?

Megnolia took a risk and decided to give her park a Fuzzy Bunnies theme. She renamed all the rides with the names of the bunny characters. Scare in the Air became the Chubby Bunny, and Bonnie's Comet became the Sugar Bunny.

Finally, the day came to unveil her new theme. Carrot burgers were sizzling in the food stands, and Fuzzy Bunnies slippers were in the souvenir stalls, waiting to be sold. The best part, Megnolia thought, were the costumed bunny characters. They looked adorable! She couldn't wait for her guests to see them.

She opened the gates and waited to hear the sounds of happy children.

Instead, she heard the sounds of their screams!

"Chubby Bunny tried to bite me!"

"Sunny Bunny stole my shoes!"

"Stinky Bunny threw a stink bomb at me!"

Megnolia thought nothing of it at first. "Poor kids," she said. "I was afraid of walk-around characters when I was young, too."

Then Megnolia heard adults screaming, and it wasn't the good screams of riders plummeting down a sixty-three-foot drop. These were real screams—truly frightened screams! The crowd rushed by her, chased by Honey Bunny and her grandfather, Big Bunny. The two were flinging rotten fruit at the fleeing customers.

"What's going on here?" Megnolia screamed. Her first thought was that the wrestlers had shown up disguised as the bunnies and were having their final revenge on her. But then Clarence came running up to her.

"Uh, boss, you need to come take a look at this," he said nervously.

They raced over to the office. A videotape of the *Fuzzy Bunnies* show was playing on the television. Megnolia watched the entire episode in horror. It seemed that during the day, the Fuzzy Bunnies were cute and sweet. But at night, the bunnies closed their grocery store and started harassing the neighborhood! They made crank phone calls, threw people's shoes at them, and flung rotten fruits and vegetables. The show wasn't cute and fuzzy at all. It was mean!

People might have enjoyed watching the show, but they definitely didn't enjoy the bunnies' crazy behavior in real life. In less than an hour's time, Megnolia's park was a disgusting mess and all the crowds had fled in fear.

After she'd finished dealing with the last angry customer, Megnolia called FB Incorporated, the company that owned the rights to the Fuzzy Bunnies characters.

"Do you *know* what your crazy rabbits did to my park!" Megnolia screamed at Devin Fryer, the president of the company.

Devin listened to Megnolia rave for five minutes before cutting her off. "Look, lady, my workers just did what they're paid to do. We sent you the tapes of the show—you knew what the Fuzzy Bunnies were all about!"

"But, but—" Megnolia stuttered.

"But nothin', " Devin growled. "And unless you wanna get sued, don't even think about trying to get out of your contract!" He slammed down the phone.

Megnolia was furious, but that was the least of

• • • • • • • •

her troubles. Her real problem became clear when she saw the late-night news that same evening. All the major networks were reporting on the fiasco in the park!

People were so turned off that for the next few days, the park had less than a hundred visitors. With hardly any customers, Megnolia was forced to close the park within a week. These days she sweeps up the peanuts outside the circus tent at Marty's Iceberg Islands park.

THE END

After calling Big Bonnie and saying "thank you" about a million times, Marty called his best friend, Stanley. Stanley was a big coaster fan just like him. Plus, he loved hearing Marty's ideas.

"Iceberg Islands sounds much better than Megnolia's crater idea," Stanley said through a mouthful of pretzels.

Marty purchased the land for the park and broke ground right away. First he built an artificial lake. Then he had five large, artificial icebergs built on the lake's surface. The icebergs looked like giant white platforms jutting out of the water. "It's just like being in the Arctic Ocean," Marty marveled proudly.

Before he could design rides, Marty had to figure out a way to get from iceberg to iceberg. Stanley suggested building a chairlift, which Marty thought was a good idea. He also built underwater tunnels so visitors could get to the icebergs on foot.

Then came the rides. Marty started with some simple favorites. There was a haunted house, complete with animated skeletons and a vampire popping out of his coffin. To keep with the icy theme, Marty built a merry-go-round with polar bears and penguins instead of carousel horses. Then he added a miniature golf course with fake snow on the ground instead of fake grass.

"You could use some more exciting rides," Stanley suggested, but Marty was already on top of it. He added a small suspended roller coaster with hanging cars called the Icicle. Riders on the Icicle had the double thrill of swinging through the air as their cars whipped around the curved track.

Finally, Marty built a roller coaster with sleek bobsled cars and called it Icy Hot. Marty gave it lots of twists and turns and blasted the riders with icy cold air to give them the sensation of sledding down a snowy mountain. Marty and Stanley were totally psyched!

Opening day arrived, and the crowd trickled in. Marty was thrilled, and Stanley was so nervous that he went through four whole bags of pretzels.

The crowds grew steadily as the weeks passed. One day, Marty said, "It's time for the next step."

Marty and Stanley debated what they should do next to expand the park and draw in the crowds.

"The coasters we have are cool," said Stanley, "but they're pretty basic. We need to build something *monster*."

It sounded like a great idea, but Marty knew that building something like that would use up the rest of the money Big Bonnie had given him. If the coaster was a flop, he'd be broke, with no way of bringing in new people.

"Maybe building kiddie rides is a better idea," Marty said. "They don't cost much, so we can build a bunch of them. They'll bring in the dough, and we can use *that* to build a really cool coaster."

"You'd better make a decision soon," Stanley reminded him. "Who knows what your sister is planning? You've got to make sure your park is the best around!"

- **If Marty decides to build kiddie rides, go to page 36.**
- **If Marty decides to build a great coaster, go to page 6.**

"No offense, Clarence, but if every park has theme characters, then I don't want them," she said. "I'd rather be unique. Let's try Lucy's idea."

Megnolia spent an entire weekend watching all the cooking shows on TV. She made a list of her favorite chefs. There was Chef Pierre, a master of French cuisine. There was Brenda Blythe, a master of Indian cuisine. And there was Carlos, a master of Mexican cuisine.

Megnolia found them all very tempting, but Mexican food was her favorite. She e-mailed Carlos at the address provided on his show.

Dear Carlos,
I run my own theme park and would love for you to provide Mexican food for my guests.
Are you interested?

Write back soon,
Megnolia Butterfield :-)

He wrote back:

Dear Megnolia,
I have just retired from food. Sorry!
Good luck.

Carlos

· · · · · · · · ·

She tried again with Chef Pierre. He responded:

> Dear Megnolia,
> Are you crazy? My gourmet food should
> only be eaten on the finest china, not on
> paper plates surrounded by buzzing flies.
> No thanks.
>
> Chef Pierre

She sent another e-mail to Brenda, who wrote back:

> Dear Megnolia,
> Sorry, but I do not find amusement parks
> at all amuse-ing.
>
> Brenda

Megnolia was furious with the snobby chefs, but she was determined not to give up. She bought a library's worth of cookbooks and spent three weeks away from the park in her kitchen trying to come up with her own gourmet amusement park food. Inspired by her corkscrew coaster, she created a superb corkscrew pasta recipe. She also invented a dish of tube-shaped pasta filled with asparagus tips, which resembled a log-flume ride.

• • • • • • • • •

When she finally returned to Crater Lake with the new menu, everyone loved the recipes she'd created. Megnolia felt triumphant, but she also felt out of place. At first she couldn't put her finger on the problem, but then it came to her. She'd lost her passion for running Crater Lake. Cooking was what she really wanted to do!

"Roller coasters are fun to ride, but the whole business is exhausting," she confessed to her staff.

She sold Crater Lake to Marty, and he merged the two parks into a megapark called Icy Lake. Megnolia opened a restaurant, which led to her own cooking show and a cookbook-publishing deal. In her spare time, she continued to create dishes exclusively for Marty's park.

THE END

. . . .

"Come on, Stanley," Marty said. "Ray Ray Pettaway directed the *Camp Fear* series. Those are the best horror movies of all time. How cool would it be to have him film a movie here? We can always do a Battle of the Bands next season."

Stanley gave in, and within a few days Ray Ray Pettaway was sitting in their office, discussing his plans for the movie.

"My film is about a young man who owns a theme park," Ray Ray said. He was a tall man who had hair like shredded wheat. His teeth were terribly crooked, and he always smiled.

"Good idea," Marty said, though he thought there had to be more than that to the movie. "What else? Is he a vampire who snacks on park visitors at night?"

"Not really," Ray Ray replied. "I don't have any more ideas yet. I thought I'd visit the park for inspiration and go from there."

Marty and Stanley gave Ray Ray a tour of the park. While they toured, they discussed ideas for a plot.

"I know I want it to be a film about roller coasters. They are symbols of life with their ups and downs, twists and turns, excitements and frights!" Ray Ray explained with a furrowed brow.

"Actually, I've been wanting to branch out a bit and try something a little different from what people expect of me. I'd like to stretch my creative muscles. It's been a lifelong dream of mine to direct a musical: *Singing in the Roller Coaster!*"

Stanley bit his lip to hold back his laughter. "But horror is what you're known for, Ray Ray. What I'd like to see is a good old Ray Ray Pettaway frightfest. Like, maybe evil aliens make the rides go out of control: *Night of the Living Roller Coaster.* You can't lose!"

Ray Ray frowned. Marty thought he'd better suggest something else.

"How about a 3-D movie?" Marty tried. "You could stretch your creativity that way. Something off the wall, with a wacky, pie-throwing fiasco at the end that will have viewers ducking and dodging. You could call it *Roller Coaster Pie Party.*"

- **What'll it be? For *Singing in the Roller Coaster*, go to page 85.**
- **For *Night of the Living Roller Coaster*, go to page 27.**
- **For *Roller Coaster Pie Party*, go to page 58.**

Megnolia looked at Lucy. "I think you're on to something," she said. "Let's build more rides than any other park in the country!"

Lucy did some research and found out that the biggest park in the country had thirty-three rides. Megnolia already had four, so to beat the record she'd have to build thirty more!

Megnolia had no idea how she was going to build so many rides with such a small staff, and Lucy, Sparky, and Clarence didn't have any ideas.

Megnolia sat on a bench overlooking her crater. She popped a piece of cinnamon gum in her mouth. She had read once that chewing gum helped get your brain moving so you could solve problems. It was worth a try.

It took five pieces of gum, but Megnolia finally found inspiration.

"A contest!" she proudly told her staff at the next meeting. "We'll start a web site and announce a contest to have coaster engineers submit their ride designs. We'll have thirty finalists and build all the winners' rides. The beauty of it is, we won't have to pay the designers! Their designs will become property of Crater Lake."

"Ahem," Lucy said, frowning.

"Don't worry, Lucy," Megnolia said quickly. "I

definitely need your help judging the entries and overseeing the construction. It's going to take a lot of work to build 30 coasters."

"Right!" Lucy said, a smile returning to her face.

Megnolia launched the web site, and the entries came pouring in. She and her staff spent four days and nights going through them. Finally, they chose the thirty best designs.

The park was plunged into chaos while the rides were built. Soon the land around Crater Lake was jammed with three steel-twister coasters, two woodies (one with a loop!), four log-flume rides, three suspended looping coasters, two launched coasters, one vertical coaster, one flying coaster, and fourteen other rides. There was barely room to move around, but Megnolia thought that just made things look more exciting.

When the park opened, Megnolia learned that her instincts had been right. Crater Lake was a hit! The park was packed.

But the money she was making from admissions wasn't enough to cover expenses. Building thirty new rides wasn't cheap. She'd already had to take a loan from the bank to get this far.

"Any suggestions about how we can keep this

park afloat?" Megnolia asked at the next staff meeting.

Sparky shrugged. "Sorry, Megnolia. We're too busy trying to keep this place running to think straight. Me and my mechanics are—"

"I know," Megnolia said. "You're working hard enough as it is."

Worrying about the park kept Megnolia up late at night. One night she was channel surfing at 3 A.M. and working on her thirteenth piece of gum when an infomercial caught her eye. She set down the remote.

"Two words, Dale—beef jerky!" an energetic man shouted on the television. "You only have to make seventy-five pounds of it and it pays for itself!" The studio audience erupted into applause.

The cogs in Megnolia's head started to churn. "Beef jerky," she said slowly. She could make her own beef jerky and serve it in the park—it was much cheaper than the pizzas and burgers she served now. She jotted down the number to order the Dale Peril Jerky Maker.

Before Megnolia could put down her pen, another infomercial started. The same energetic announcer was yelling about a "revolutionary new lawn care product—Dale Peril's Growth Spurt

Stunter!" A tall, bald man who Megnolia guessed was Dale Peril was holding up a green container and waving at the audience.

Megnolia watched, transfixed. The Growth-Spurt Stunter would keep the grass from growing. That meant no more grass to mow!

"That's perfect," Megnolia said. "I can let go of all the guys on Clarence's team. I'll save so much money in salaries."

Then she frowned. "Too bad I can't afford to buy the jerky makers and the growth stunter. I wonder which one I should get."

- **If Megnolia decides to buy the beef jerky maker, go to page 79.**
- **If Megnolia buys the Growth-Spurt Stunter, go to page 55.**

Marty took out a loan for just five hundred thousand dollars and planned to pay it back within six months.

"Chief, I think you should use this money to design a Steel Mouse Coaster—you know, those old-fashioned coasters with cars shaped like mice? They don't make them anymore, so they'll be new to kids and for their parents it'll be just like reliving their childhood memories." Stanley was really learning his way around the business.

"That sounds great," Marty said. "We'll build it higher, faster, and longer than any mouse coaster in the world. Then we'll move on to the three-hundred-sixty degrees coaster."

That's exactly what they did. The Steel Mouse Coaster was a success, and Marty repaid the loan. Then they started to work on the three-hundred-sixty degrees ride. Marty called it 360 Degrees Below Zero.

The new ride opened the next season, and it was a huge hit.

"Three-hundred-sixty Degrees is the ultimate ride!"

"Marty Butterfield is a genius!"

"Megnolia Butterfield should take lessons from her brother—her park bites!"

• • • • • • • • •

When Marty heard this last comment, he had another idea and called Megnolia.

She answered the phone in tears. "Oh, Marty! People hate my park. They think it's boring. They throw popcorn at me whenever they see me. At this point, I'd rather ride the dumb rides than design them."

Marty genuinely felt bad for his sister, but her confession only made him feel better about his idea. "I'm sorry, Megnolia, really," he said. "But I might have a solution to your problem. Why don't you sell me your park? My park's doing great and I really want to expand."

Megnolia hated to admit defeat, but she was sick of trying to run a theme park.

"Fine," she said. "Whatever. Work it out with my lawyers. I'm going on vacation."

For Marty, having two parks meant twice the work, but it also meant twice the excitement, twice the fun, and, ultimately, twice the success.

Under Marty's management, both parks continued to expand physically until they actually met and he owned one gigantic megapark.

He let Megnolia come any time she wanted— for free, of course.

THE END

"You know, I think a haunted house is a pretty cool idea," Megnolia said. "We'll make it the scariest, freakiest haunted house in the world— people will never get tired of it!"

So Megnolia went to work on the haunted house, getting Kenny to help her make it as scary as possible. They built a dungeon in the basement, populated by flesh-eating ghouls. Maniacs with fake chainsaws chased visitors through the hallways. And every dark corner in the house hid secret compartments so that costumed actors could pop out and surprise people.

When the haunted house was almost finished, Kenny blanketed the town with advertising fliers. Shortly after, Megnolia received a phone call.

"Megnolia Butterfield?" asked a voice with a thick accent. "This is Count Von Vamp!"

The name sounded familiar. "Aren't you, like, famous or something?" Megnolia asked.

"Silly child! I am the most famous television horror host to ever live...or die," he cackled in a creepy voice.

"Of course!" Megnolia exclaimed. "My brother watches your show *Dread Night* all the time! How can I help you, Count?" she asked.

"I saw a flier for your new haunted house," he

said. "I would be the perfect addition for your attraction! I could greet visitors as they enter…for a fee, of course."

The idea sounded good to Megnolia. Having a celebrity working at the park could bring in lots of new customers.

Then again, Crater Lake already had quite enough colorful characters—her wrestling friends. She wasn't sure there was room in the park for even just one more man in makeup!

- **If Megnolia agrees to hire Count Von Vamp, go to page 89.**
- **If Megnolia turns down the Count, go to page 68.**

"I guess you're right," Marty admitted. "I'm in this for the coasters, not the food. And *I* don't have to eat it."

Marty got to work right away. He built three burger joints, two pizza places, and two hot dog stands. Of course, people loved them.

As Marty walked through the park, he had to weave his way in and out of the crowd. He over-heard bits of people's conversations.

"The hamburgers here are even better than my dad's!"

"Let's ride the Abominable again. But I need a slice of pizza first."

"This is the fourth hot dog I've had since I got here—yum!"

"I'm feeling nauseous, but I gotta have one more burger—and then one more round of Icy Hot!"

Marty couldn't believe how successful the park was. The food stands were bringing in a nice profit. Combined with the profits he made from the Abominable Snow Coaster, he had plenty of extra cash.

"So Tycoon, you're doing great! You should expand," Stanley suggested.

"You're right, Stanley!" Marty agreed.

. . . .

Marty didn't wait. He went on a designing spree. He built a super-fast hyper-coaster and a suspended coaster twice as big as the Icicle. He added a corkscrew coaster that took riders on endless twists and turns. Then he finished with a river-rapids ride that sent riders plunging thirty feet into a pool of cold water.

"Great rides and great food are the perfect combination," Marty told Stanley proudly on the day the new rides opened. "I've spent all of my money on the new rides, but I should earn it all right back."

Marty and Stanley walked around the park, checking out reactions to the rides. He wasn't prepared for what he saw.

Men, women, and children stumbled off the rides, their faces pale green.

"I shouldn't have eaten those three hot dogs before riding the rapids," one man was saying. "Next time I'll—*blaaaaaarp!*"

That's when the vomit started flying. It was like a chain reaction. A little girl puked up pepperoni pizza. A grandma coughed up a double cheese-burger. Soon the lunches of six thousand people were floating in the icy lake.

"You were right, Marty," Stanley said. "Great

rides and lots great, greasy food *is* the perfect combination—for puke!"

Marty and Stanley ran for cover. They huddled inside the spiral slide, the sound of retching echoing in their ears.

"How are we going to clean this up?" Stanley moaned.

"It's going to take a lot of water, a lot of time, a lot of air freshener—and a lot of money," Marty said. "In fact, all of my money. I think I've been puked out of business!"

THE END

Megnolia walked up to Star Crunch and put her arm around his shoulder.

"Listen, Star Crunch," she said. "I'm sorry I didn't use any of your ideas. It's just that I have this whole new theme in mind for the park. I'd like to keep it a surprise. But I know you guys will like it. Give me a few weeks, okay? In the meantime, I'll give your wrestlers free admission every Tuesday until it's done."

Star Crunch nodded. "It's a deal," he said.

The free rides kept the wrestlers content for a while. In the meantime, Megnolia and Lucy worked feverishly on the new theme.

Finally, they were ready to unveil the new and improved park. Megnolia invited Star Crunch and the wrestlers to the park on opening day.

"Presenting, Peaceful Planet!" Megnolia announced, tearing a sheet off of the new park sign.

The wrestlers mumbled to each other, confused.

"It's our new groovy theme, man," she said. "Come on, you'll love it."

Megnolia gave the wrestlers a tour of the park. She had built a new triple-looped coaster called Hippie Dippy. She'd added a Ferris wheel designed to look like a peace sign. She renamed Bonnie's Comet as Flower Power. The souvenir stands sold love beads, and the drink stands sold soothing herbal tea.

"Meggie, I hate to disappoint you, but this place is boring," Star Crunch said, yawning.

"You said it," Dreadful Dog agreed.

Megnolia pretended to frown. "That's too bad, guys," she said. "I thought you'd like it." Then she brightened. "Hey, I hear my brother Marty's park is pretty exciting. Why don't you guys check out Iceberg Islands?"

"Sounds great!" said Star Crunch.

That was the last Megnolia saw of the wrestlers. Now her park was populated by hippies, but she didn't mind. They wore funny clothes, too, but she never saw any of them perform a single body slam!

THE END

Read the next book in the RollerCoaster Tycoon™ Pick Your Path! series!

THE FRIENDS: Jason and Max, aka The Dynamic Coaster Duo.

THE PROBLEM: Mysterious stuff is going on at the local theme park. Really scary stuff. Downright *freaky* stuff.

THE QUESTION: Is it just a run of bad luck? Or is it sabotage? Can you help Jason and Max get to the bottom of it all— before it's too late?

The choice is yours!